CTW
SESAME STREET

A
Sesame Street
Christmas

Written by PAT TORNBORG
Illustrated by TOM COOKE

A SESAME STREET / MERRIGOLD PRESS BOOK
Published by Merrigold Press
in conjunction with Children's Television Workshop

Christmas was just a week away and it was raining when I splashed into the park. I found the gang from Sesame Street gathered under Big Bird's umbrella.

"Why all the long faces?" I asked.

"I can't build my Bert snow man," said Ernie.

"I can't count the snowflakes," said the Count.

"Me no eat snow cones," said Cookie Monster.

And then everyone nodded and looked miserable. So, I said, "This is just great! Nobody has any of that Christmas spirit they're always nagging me about! It's going to be a damp and gloomy holiday, after all. Whoopee!"

But Betty Lou didn't agree with me. She said, "Not so fast, Oscar! We're not giving up on Christmas spirit yet! Come on, everybody. Let's go to my house for some milk and cookies."

Aw, all this Christmas spirit jazz is making me sick. Big Bird, you take over.

Sure, Oscar. So we went to Betty Lou's house and everyone ate six cookies, and drank two glasses of milk, and felt a little cheerier.

"Who cares about the rain?" said Bert.

"Let's have a terrific Christmas, anyway!" said Ernie.

"Let's sing Christmas carols and tell stories!" said Betty Lou.

I said, "Sure! I can read you a Christmas poem right now. My Granny Bird reads it to me every Christmas. It's about the time there was too much snow for Christmas. Listen."

THE NIGHT BEFORE CHRISTMAS ON SESAME STREET

'Twas the night before Christmas on Sesame Street.
And a stormy one, too, with the snow and the sleet!
All the kids in the neighborhood, snug in pajamas,
Were saying good-night to their papas and mamas.

The house was all quiet at Ernie and Bert's,
As they climbed into bed in their cozy nightshirts.
And even outside, everyone was at rest—
The grouch in his can and I in my nest.

There was one little house where not all was so comfy—
'Twas the home of that famous magician named Mumfie.
He feared that the blizzard would keep Santa away,
And he thought of a bleak Christmas morn with dismay.

"This storm might be too much for Santa," he said,
"So I'll conjure some toys for the children instead."
Then he snatched up his wand, and before he could say,
"A la Peanut Butter Sandwiches!" he was on his way.

A little past midnight, Ernie jumped out of bed.
He'd been jolted awake by a "thump" overhead.
As he peered at the roof, he said, "Gee, Bert, that's funny.
I thought Santa had reindeer, but that looks like a bunny!"

Ernie raced to the living room, just as a foot
Had emerged from the chimney all covered with soot.
The body that followed was equally grubby.
Said Ernie, "Why, this Santa's not even chubby!

"His face is all dirty, his cloak's black as night.
But I always thought Santa wore red and white!
He has only a stick poking out of his pouch,
And these gifts should have gone to Oscar the Grouch!"

Ernie hopped back in bed and was soon sound asleep,
But poor Mumford had other appointments to keep.
With his team of white rabbits, the brave little wizard
Continued his trip through the terrible blizzard.

Mumfie's magic did wonders on that Christmas Eve,
But the gifts it created were hard to believe!
There was seed for a bird by the Count's Christmas tree,
And the sneakers for me were only size three!

Little Grover had hoped for a new teddy bear,
But his gift was a ribbon for Betty Lou's hair.
And if you think that Grover was pretty unlucky,
Bert's soap dish was intended for poor Rubber Duckie!

As the morning came, Mumford drove home through
    the drifts.
He had made all his rounds, given everyone gifts.
So imagine his shock when he walked in to see
A fat, jolly old man sitting there by his tree!

"Mumford, my friend," Santa said with a smile,
"I've been two steps behind you for quite a long while.
Though you made some unusual gift selections,
You've done a fine job (with my little corrections).

"I followed your sleigh and erased all your traces.
You left all the right gifts, but in all the wrong places!
I just made a few switches, so no one would know
That old Santa Claus was held up by the snow.

"But the meaning of Christmas is not gifts, my boy;
It's the impulse to do things that bring others joy!
Though your magical wand can't do anything right,
The true magic of Christmas was with you tonight!"

With a nod of his head and a wink of his eye,
Santa hopped in his sleigh and took off for the sky.
He was heard to exclaim, as he flew out of sight,
        "A LA PEANUT BUTTER SANDWICHES!
            AND TO ALL, A GOOD-NIGHT!"

When I finished reading the poem,
Betty Lou said, "Thanks for that poem,
Big Bird. Now I'm not worried about the rain or the snow."
Then Grover said, "Oh, neither am I! Christmas is
Christmas, whatever the weather!"
And I think Grover was right. Don't you?

No, Bird, I don't think
Grover was right.
Christmas is much better
when the weather is
crummy! Anyhow, I've
got my own Christmas
story to tell. I call it
"Oscar's Christmas Carol
(A Dickens of a Story)."
Now, listen!

OSCAR'S CHRISTMAS CAROL
(A Dickens of a Story)

"BAH, HUMBUG!" I said loudly, just as Big Bird and Betty Lou walked by. "BAH, HUMBUG!" I said again, as they stopped to stare.

"Whatever that means, it sure sounds grouchy!" said Betty Lou. "What's the matter, Oscar?"

"Nothing's the matter," I answered. "Everything's great. I'm reading a terrific story about a mean old fellow named Mr. Scrooge. He hated Christmas, so he said, 'Bah, Humbug!' all the time. He sounds just like my uncle Smarmy. Why, he might even be a relative of mine!"

"How could anyone hate Christmas?" asked Betty Lou. "Everyone is good and kind at Christmas, and there are good things to eat, and songs to sing, and presents to give. Christmas is a happy time, Oscar."

"Bah, Humbug!" I replied.

"Mr. Scrooge had a way of fixing that. Not only was he miserable himself, but he ruined everyone else's Christmas, too. He even made his helper, Bob Cratchit, work on Christmas Eve! Boy, that's a real grouch for you!"

"Hey, wait a minute," said Bird. "I know that story. It's 'A Christmas Carol,' by Mr. Charles Dickens. Maria read it to me last Christmas. And guess what, Oscar? It has a happy ending!"

"How could it?" I asked. I was disgusted. "This guy Scrooge was such a great grouch! He's my hero—an inspiration! I want to be just like him."

"Well, then," said Bird, "you'll have to stop being a grouch, because that's what Scrooge did. He had a dream that showed him how wrong he had been about Christmas. You should read the rest of the book, Oscar."

And I said, "BAH, HUMBUG!" as I disappeared into my trash can.

I HATE CHRISTMAS

I can't think of anything that's dumber;
To a grouch, Christmas is a bummer.

Beaming faces everywhere,
Happiness is in the air.
I'm telling you it isn't fair.
I hate Christmas!

People loaded with good will,
Giving presents—what a thrill!
That slushy nonsense makes me ill.
I hate Christmas!

I'd rather have a holiday
Like normal grouches do.
Instead of getting presents,
They take presents back from you!

Here comes Santa, girls and boys.
So who needs that big red noise?
I'll tell him where to leave his toys.
I hate Christmas!
(And if you want the truth, I ain't so crazy
about Easter and Labor Day, either!)

Christmas carols to be sung,
Decorations to be hung.
Oh yeah, well I stick out my tongue!
I hate Christmas!

Christmas bells play loud and strong,
Hurts my ears, all that ding-dong.
Besides, it goes on much too long!
I hate Christmas!

I'd rather have a holiday
With a lot less joy and flash.
With a lot less cheerful smiling
And a lot more dirty trash. Yeah!

Christmas Day is almost here.
When it's over, then I cheer.
I'm glad it's only once a year!
I hate Christmas!

And whoever hung that mistletoe
over my trashcan, Well, I say,
"PHOOEY and BAH, HUMBUG!"

A little later, Bird passed my trash can on his way home from Betty Lou's house. I shouted, "Merry Christmas, Bird!" as I popped out of the can.

So, Bird looked at me in surprise. He said, "Why, Oscar, you changed your mind. You must have had a dream, just like Mr. Scrooge did. And now, you're not going to be a grouch anymore!"

And I said, "Ho, ho, ho. No, no, no! That's not what happened. I was giving that silly book with the happy ending to the trash man just after you left, and he reminded me that Christmas is a holiday. Do you know what that means, Bird?"

Bird answered, "Sure. A holiday is a day when everyone is good and kind and celebrates...."

I had to interrupt. "No, no! It means that there's no trash pick-up that day, and I get to keep my wonderful trash one more day! What a gift! Merry Christmas, Bird!"

Gee, Oscar, that was a really grouchy story. Christmas isn't a grouchy time. It's a merry time! So let me tell a happy story, because that's what Christmas is all about! Here it is. It's called "A Wrap Session."

A WRAP SESSION

Early one Christmas Eve, not so long ago, everyone on Sesame Street gathered to wrap presents before the big Christmas party. But nobody had remembered to bring any wrapping paper or ribbons! Just then, Oscar the Grouch arrived with his gifts all wrapped up in newspaper and tied with bits of old string.

Betty Lou said, "Hey, Oscar, what a good idea! We don't need fancy paper and ribbons. We can wrap our presents with all kinds of things we find around the house!"

Just as we were finishing wrapping the gifts, Prairie Dawn looked out the window. She cried, "Oh, look! It's snowing! It's going to be a white Christmas after all! Let's go caroling!"

And that's just what we did. Here's what we sang.

GIFTS FOR THE TWELVE DAYS OF CHRISTMAS

FIRST DAY ....1 Delicious Cookie

SECOND DAY..........2 Baby Frogs

THIRD DAY ....3 Footballs

FOURTH DAY..........4 Woolly Bears

FIFTH DAY ....5 Argyle Socks

SIXTH DAY.............6 Rubber Duckies

SEVENTH DAY ....7 Rusty Trash Cans

EIGHTH DAY ....8 Counts a-Counting

NINTH DAY.............9 Pounds of Birdseed

TENTH DAY ....10 Wind-up Rabbits

ELEVENTH DAY......11 Broken Buildings

TWELFTH DAY ....?

MERRY CHRISTMAS,
EVERYBODY!

HAVE A GROUCHY
CHRISTMAS!

THE END!